Adventure/Fantasy

The *Last* of the *Mohicans*

by James Fenimore Cooper
adapted by Les Martin

*H*eyward moved back toward Natty. He took a paddle. Soon he picked up Natty's rhythm. The silence was broken only by the rippling water. Then came a distant roaring.

Heyward looked over the side. The water was swirling. Rocks jutted through white foam.

The roaring grew louder.

Heyward turned his eyes forward. He sucked in his breath.

A giant waterfall was dead ahead. The canoe was heading straight for it.

Fifty feet more and the waterfall would hit them. Crush them. Drown them all.

Les Martin is the author and adapter of many books for children, including two other Stepping Stones Classics, *The Time Machine* and *Oliver Twist*. An avid tennis player, Les Martin lives in New York City.

Shannon Stirnweis is a painter and illustrator with dozens of books to his credit. He likes to paint wilderness scenes, so he especially enjoyed working on *The Last of the Mohicans*. Born in Oregon, Shannon Stirnweis now lives in Wilton, Connecticut, with his wife and son.

The Last of the Mohicans

by James Fenimore Cooper
adapted by Les Martin
illustrated by Shannon Stirnweis

A STEPPING STONE BOOK™
Random House 🏠 New York

www.steppingstonesbooks.com

Library of Congress Cataloging-in-Publication Data
Martin, Les, 1934–
The last of the Mohicans / by James Fenimore Cooper ; adapted by Les Martin ;
illustrated by Shannon Stirnweis.
    p.   cm.
"A Stepping Stone book."
SUMMARY: A simplified retelling of the classic tale set in 1757 about the exploits
of Hawkeye, a colonial scout, and his friends Chingachgook, a chief of the
Mohicans, and his son Uncas during the French and Indian War.
ISBN 0-679-84706-5 (pbk.) — ISBN 0-679-99434-3 (lib. bdg.)
1. United States—History—French and Indian War, 1755–1763—Juvenile fiction.
2. Mohegan Indians—Juvenile fiction. [1. United States—History—French and
Indian War, 1755–1763—Fiction. 2. Mohegan Indians—Fiction. 3. Indians of
North America—East (U.S.)—Fiction. 4. Frontier and pioneer life—Fiction.]
I. Stirnweis, Shannon, ill. II. Cooper, James Fenimore, 1789–1851. Last of the
Mohicans. III. Title.   PZ7.M36353Las 2005   [Fic]—dc22   2004009364

Printed in the United States of America   25 24 23 22 21 20 19 18 17 16

Chapter 1

Major Duncan Heyward was a brave young British officer. He had fought well for his country in Europe.

Now he was far from Europe. But he was still serving his country. He was in North America, where the forces of England fought those of France.

Each side had settlements there. The French controlled the eastern part of Canada. They called it New France. Below New France, England had colonies down the Atlantic coast to Georgia. Both countries claimed the vast territory to the west. That was what they were fighting for.

This was a new kind of war for Major Heyward. There were no open battlefields. There were no great armies facing each other. The two sides fought in a wilderness of forests, rivers, and lakes. Each side used native American Indians as well as its own troops.

So far, the French were better than the English at this warfare. Their leader, General Montcalm, had fewer soldiers than the English. But he knew how to fight in the wilderness. He moved swiftly on the lakes and rivers. He fought from the cover of the forests. And he had many more Indians on his side. Now, in 1757, he was on the attack. He wanted to destroy the forts that the English had built.

Major Heyward was on his way to one of those forts. Fort William Henry, on the shore of Lake George, was under threat of attack. But Heyward had no soldiers with him. He was with two young women. They rode on horseback along a twisting forest path. Ahead of them an Indian guide moved on foot.

The young women were sisters, but they looked as different as night and day.

One had dark hair and dark eyes. Her name was Cora. The other was blond and blue-eyed. Her name was Alice.

They were different in other ways, too. Cora was bold and spirited. She said what she thought and did what she thought was best. Alice was gentle and sweet tempered. She put her trust in the goodness of others. She

put her fate in their hands.

The sisters loved each other. They loved their father as well. They were on their way to join him. He was Colonel Munro, who commanded Fort William Henry.

"I wish you did not insist on joining your father," Heyward said to them as they slowly rode along. "It is much too dangerous. Even now the French may be attacking the fort. Enemy Indians may be roaming these woods."

"Nonsense," said Cora. "You said yourself that no one would notice us. That's why you sent your soldiers marching to the fort along the main road—so they would draw the attention of any enemies."

"Besides, I always feel safe with you, Duncan," Alice said. Her blue eyes gazed into his gray ones.

"I thought this way would be safe," said Heyward. "But now——"

He stopped abruptly. He saw that their Indian guide was listening. He knew that the Indian understood English. So Heyward could not say aloud what he feared. He trusted the Indian less and less as they moved deeper and deeper into the forest.

We should be near the fort by now, Heyward thought. But there was no sign of it.

Then, suddenly, Heyward forgot his vague suspicions.

He was face to face with real danger.

On the path three men appeared as if from nowhere. All held rifles at the ready.

Chapter 2

Major Heyward kept his face calm. But his hand went to his pistol.

He did not know what to make of the three men in his path. He was taking no chances.

One of them was white. His face, though, was burned nut-brown from the sun. He was tall and lean. He wore a hunting shirt of forest green and buckskin pants. On his feet were Indian moccasins decorated with beads. On his head was a hat of animal skin shorn of fur. His long dark hair hung down below the hat. In his hands was the longest rifle Heyward had ever seen.

Slightly behind him stood two Indians. Their rifles were far shorter. Tomahawks were tucked into loincloths around their middles. Otherwise the Indians were naked. Their heads were shaved, except for tufts of hair in the center. Heyward knew why Indians wore those tufts. They were prizes for any enemy who beat them in battle. Indians took scalps as trophies of victory.

When Heyward first arrived in America, all Indians had looked alike to him. But by now he could tell them apart.

He saw that one of the Indians was middle-aged but still strong as a bull. The Indian had an air of power. He looked like a man born to command.

The other Indian was younger, twenty perhaps. His face was noble.

His body reminded Heyward of statues of Greek gods in museums. He was the most splendid Indian that Heyward had ever seen.

Heyward opened his mouth to question the three. But the white stranger spoke first.

"Who are you?" the man demanded.

Heyward relaxed. He had feared that this man was French. Many French lived on close terms with Indians. But this man spoke perfect English.

"I am Duncan Heyward, major in His Majesty's army," Heyward answered.

"And what might you be doing here?" the stranger went on.

Heyward held up his hand. "Before I tell you more, who are *you*?"

The stranger smiled. "I go by different names. Indian foes call me the Long Rifle. Indian friends call me Hawkeye."

"And your English name?" asked Heyward.

"Natty Bumppo," the man said. "The name my parents gave me before they died."

"And who are the Indians?" asked Heyward.

Natty gestured toward the older Indian. "This is Chingachgook, who raised me like a son."

He turned toward the younger one. "This is Uncas, son of Chingachgook. He is like a younger brother to me."

"What is their tribe?" Heyward demanded. He had to know which side of the war they were on.

"They are Mohicans," Natty said.

Heyward was puzzled. "I've never heard of such a tribe."

Natty nodded. "Not surprising. Yet once the Mohicans were the greatest of tribes. The proudest, the purest, the most ancient. They came from the west. They won the eastern coast from the Iroquois. They ruled the Delaware Indian nation."

"What happened to them?" Heyward asked, fascinated.

"The white men happened to them," Natty said. Behind him Chingachgook nodded, his face stonelike.

"The white men gave them whiskey that robbed them of their strength," Natty went on. "Diseases that robbed them of their health. Trinkets that robbed them of their land."

Again Chingachgook nodded.

"Now only two of the tribe are

left," Natty said. "Chingachgook, last chief of the Mohicans. And Uncas, his son."

"A sad story," said Cora Munro, who had been listening. She looked at Chingachgook with respect. Her gaze traveled to Uncas. He answered her gaze with his. Both found it hard to turn their eyes away.

Natty's voice broke the spell. "Now, Major, what are you doing in this forest?"

"I am taking these two ladies to their father at Fort William Henry," Heyward said. "He is the commander there."

"And who told you to come this way?" Natty asked.

"Our Indian guide, Magua," said Heyward, lowering his voice. The guide had sat down under a tree a good distance away. But Heyward knew how sharp his Indian guide's hearing could be.

Natty lowered his voice as well. "His tribe?"

"The Mohawks, our friends," Heyward replied.

Chingachgook gave the guide a quick look. He slowly shook his head. Natty nodded in agreement.

"Are you *sure* he's a Mohawk?" Natty demanded.

"Once he was a Huron," Heyward admitted. "But he joined the Mohawks when he came south from Canada."

For the first time Chingachgook spoke. "Once a Huron, always a Huron."

"But—" said Heyward.

"There is no time for buts," Natty said urgently. "I just hope there is time to save your lives."

Chapter 3

"Time to save our lives?" said Heyward. "What do you mean?"

"Yes, tell us," Cora Munro said.

"Please," her sister Alice said.

But Natty had already turned to Chingachgook and Uncas. He spoke in Mohican to them. They nodded, then faded into the forest.

Natty turned back to Heyward. "Your guide has taken you in the wrong direction. He is leading you into a trap."

"Perhaps he made a wrong turn," Heyward said.

"No Indian gets lost in the woods," Natty said. "His friends must be hiding nearby. Listen to me. Go to him. Convince him you suspect nothing. Chingachgook and Uncas will sneak up on him. We can hold him hostage and be safe from attack."

"I'll capture him myself," Heyward said. He had a soldier's pride.

"He'd kill you the moment you got off your horse." Natty shrugged.

Heyward did not argue. The guide Magua was tall and strong. He looked as if he could move like lightning.

Heyward rode to where Magua sat.

"The hunter says the fort is still far away," Heyward said. "The ladies are tired. We'll rest here for the night."

Magua's lips curled with contempt for the white man's worrying about women. His eyes glowed with anger.

"You trust that white man more than me? Then let him be your guide."

"Don't be foolish. I know you are the best of guides," soothed Heyward. He reached into his saddle pouch. He took out a packet of dried corn. "Here is a good evening meal for you."

Magua reached up to take it. But instead he grabbed Heyward's arm. He gave a vicious yank. As Heyward fell from his horse, Magua leaped to his feet. He vanished into the forest.

There was a loud shot. Heyward, on his hands and knees, turned toward Natty. Natty's long rifle was smoking.

"He moved too fast—even for my deerslayer here," Natty muttered.

Chingachgook and Uncas came out of the forest. They joined Natty in hunting Magua's trail. Heyward tagged along.

Natty pointed to a sumac bush. "These leaves should be yellow now in July, but they are stained red. Blood red."

"You hit him!" Heyward said.

Natty shook his head. "Just grazed him. The kind of wound that makes an animal run faster. Otherwise we'd have found his body."

Natty peered into the forest. It was easy to see why he was called Hawkeye.

"The Huron will return with his friends. We have to get out of here," Natty said. He headed back to Cora and Alice. "Ladies, get off your horses."

"Why should they?" asked Heyward.

"Horses leave too clear a trail,"

Natty said. "The Hurons will be hunting us."

"But what will you do with them?" Heyward asked.

"Perhaps the best thing would be to kill them," Natty said.

Alice gasped. "Never! I have had my horse since I was a child. I love him."

Cora cut in firmly, "We must listen to Mr. Bumppo. Our lives are in his hands. This is a savage land. He knows how to survive in it."

Cora got off her horse. Alice's eyes brimmed with tears, but she followed. Heyward could not stand to see Alice cry. "I will not let you kill the horses," he declared.

Natty's voice was hard. "If you want to live, you must follow my orders, Major. Understood?"

Heyward bit his lip. He was an officer of the Crown. But he was like a child in this wilderness. "Understood."

Natty looked at the horses again. "Maybe we should not kill them. No sense telling the Hurons we are on foot. Instead Chingachgook and Uncas can hide them. Tomorrow you can use them. I will tell you how to get to the fort. In daylight you can ride fast enough to make it there."

Natty looked at his Indian friends. They nodded. The plan was settled.

Natty and the Mohicans led the horses through the forest. They moved swiftly. Alice, Cora, and Heyward struggled to keep up with them.

The sun had set. A full moon had risen. Through ghostly trees a river shimmered silver.

They reached the river. It was shallow near its bank. The Mohicans led the horses splashing upstream.

"The Hurons cannot follow a trail in the water," Natty said. "My friends will hide the horses well. Meanwhile, we will go to our hiding place."

Natty pulled aside thick bushes. A canoe was hidden there. Natty slid it into the water and pointed to the front. Heyward and the women sat there. Natty pushed it off and got in back. He picked up a paddle. It bit into the water with smooth power.

Heyward moved back toward Natty. He took a paddle. Soon he picked up Natty's rhythm. The silence was broken only by the rippling water. Then came a distant roaring.

Heyward looked over the side. The water was swirling. Rocks jutted through white foam.

The roaring grew louder.

Heyward turned his eyes forward. He sucked in his breath.

A giant waterfall was dead ahead. The canoe was heading straight for it.

Fifty feet more and the waterfall would hit them. Crush them. Drown them all.

Chapter 4

Heyward stopped paddling. But Natty kept on. Was he mad?

They came closer to the falls. Now Heyward could see where they were going. He started paddling again.

The waterfall came down in two huge streams. Between them was a gap. In that gap was the mouth of a cave. On a stone ledge in front of it the Mohicans were waiting.

The canoe moved through a cloud of spray. It reached the ledge. Natty and the others climbed out. The Mohicans climbed in. They had tethered the horses behind the wall of falling water. They would hide the canoe downstream.

Natty led the others into the cave. With a flint he lit a brushwood fire. He hung a blanket over the entrance so no one outside could spot the light. Soon Chingachgook and Uncas returned.

"Only we know of this place," Natty said. "We will be safe for a night."

"But what if you're wrong?" said Heyward. He refused to follow Natty blindly. This man was not even a soldier, much less an officer. "If the Hurons find us, we'll be trapped."

Natty smiled. "A fox never chooses a lair with only one escape. There is a way out in the back. Even better, the cave is divided into two parts. I'll show you."

Natty went to the rear of the cave.

He parted a pile of brushwood. A second cave was hidden behind. It was a perfect hideout from intruders.

They settled down for the night. The women huddled under their shawls. The Mohicans guarded the entrance. Heyward sat by Natty near the fire.

"The Mohicans' names—what do they mean?" asked Heyward.

"Chingachgook means 'Great Serpent,'" said Natty.

"A snake? Not very nice," said Heyward.

"Among the Indians it is," explained Natty. "It means he knows the twists and turns of human nature. And he can strike at any weakness."

"And Uncas?" asked Heyward.

"'Running Deer,'" said Natty. "Indeed, he is as swift and brave as a young stag."

"I should have paid more attention to Indian names," said Heyward. "Our false guide told me what his name meant: 'Cunning Fox.'"

"Magua is one, all right," said Natty. "But now let me ask you something. Why are you taking these women to Fort William Henry? It is in danger."

"I can answer that," said Alice. She had been listening. "I sent my father a letter. I begged him to let us join him. We missed him so very much."

"He never can say no to Alice," Cora added. "I should have, though. Since our mother's death I have been both sister and mother to her. But I, too, longed to see Father again."

Natty shrugged. "With luck, you

will. But after that—who knows?"

For a moment, there was silence.

Then a hideous sound came from the night outside.

Natty leaped to his feet. He went to the cave entrance. Heyward followed.

The sound came again.

Natty was puzzled. "I thought I knew all the forest sounds. But not this one."

Chingachgook and Uncas shook their heads.

"I know what it is," Heyward said grimly. "I have heard it on battlefields. It is a horse in agony."

Natty's mouth tightened. "Wolves have found the horses."

Alice gasped—and began to cry.

"No time for tears," said Natty. "Try to get a little sleep. The Hurons have sharp ears. They will know where to hunt. We must be out of here by dawn."

"Why not leave now?" asked Cora.

"You need rest," said Natty. "We have to travel long and fast on foot tomorrow."

"Natty is right, Cora," said Heyward. "Alice is not as strong as you."

"I must admit I *am* tired," Alice said.

"You need rest as well, Major," Natty said. "The Mohicans and I will stand guard tonight."

Heyward started to argue. But he could not deny that his eyelids were heavy. He decided to close them for a moment.

It seemed a moment later that he was shaken awake.

"It's dawn," Natty said. "So far the Hurons haven't shown themselves."

The east was brightening as they

left the cave. The fading moon hung low.

Natty had Heyward and the women wait on the stone ledge. The Mohicans went to scout the nearby woods. Natty went to fetch supplies from the canoe. Above all, he wanted the extra gunpowder in it. He feared he might need it before the day was over.

Heyward saw Alice trembling. He tried to reassure her. "All we need is a little luck and we'll be—"

He didn't finish the sentence. War whoops and rifle shots ended it.

Chapter 5

Chingachgook and Uncas burst from the woods. They started running over the rocks behind the falls. It was the only way to reach the ledge in front of the cave.

Behind them Hurons appeared. One aimed a rifle at Chingachgook's back. Another rifle fired first. The Huron fell face forward into the water.

Heyward saw Natty standing on the other riverbank. His long rifle was hunting other targets. But the Hurons had retreated.

Soon Natty and the Mohicans had rejoined Heyward and the women.

"Superb shooting," Heyward said to Natty. "You've driven them away."

"Thanks to my deerslayer," Natty said. He patted his long rifle fondly. Then his face darkened. "The Hurons will be back—in force. We've drawn blood. They'll hunger for revenge."

"Then they will fall before your rifle," Cora said. She looked at Natty with admiration.

Natty shook his head glumly. Then he shook his powder horn. "Not much powder left," he said. "I didn't get to the canoe. The Huron attack came too fast."

Heyward looked downstream. His mouth dropped open. "Look," he exclaimed. "There's the canoe now."

The canoe was moving upstream

toward them. Yet there was no one paddling it.

Natty saw what Heyward had not. He raised his rifle again. His shot ripped through the canoe. There was a cry of pain. Heyward saw naked Hurons swimming desperately away. They had been pushing the canoe ahead of them for cover.

Natty watched the canoe drift away. "There goes the gunpowder. Come on. Follow me."

He climbed the rocks between the two parts of the falls. The others followed. Heyward was the last to get to the top. He stayed behind Cora and Alice. He wanted to be sure they made it.

Heyward could now see why the waterfall was divided. On the top was a tree-covered island.

A shot rang out. It seemed to

come from nowhere. They all dived for cover.

Crouched behind a tree, Natty spied the spent bullet. Instantly his eyes scanned the treetops. A moment later his long rifle fired. A Huron dropped like ripe fruit from a high branch.

Natty answered the question in Heyward's eyes. "I saw how the Huron bullet was flattened. It had to have come from above."

That was all he got to say. Four Huron warriors broke through the underbrush. Natty, the Mohicans, and Heyward met them.

Heyward thrust his sword at a huge Huron. But the Indian dodged. The sword snapped like a twig against a tree. Just in time Heyward grabbed the Indian's knife hand by the wrist. He bent the wrist back.

The knife dropped to the ground. Heyward and the Huron grappled at the top of the falls. It was a test of pure strength.

Inch by inch Heyward was forced backward. In a moment he would go plunging to his death.

Suddenly the Huron loosened his grip. Blood spurted from his wrist. Uncas had come racing to Heyward's aid. The knife of Running Deer had saved Heyward's life. Heyward gave a desperate push. The Huron went screaming over the edge.

Heyward looked around. The other Hurons all lay dead.

"More will be here any minute," Natty said. "Quick. Back to the cave."

Inside the cave Heyward said, "We can hold them off here. It will be easy to defend the entrance."

Natty grimaced. "With what?" He

shook his powder horn. It was empty.

Then Cora spoke. "Please, Mr. Bumppo, you and your Indian friends save yourselves. It is not fair that you risk your lives for ours."

Natty's face clouded. He spoke in Mohican to his friends. Then he turned back to Cora. "You're right. We stand a chance of escaping down-river."

Heyward's heart sank. But he was not surprised. He could not expect more from this hunter and the Mohicans. They were little more than savages. Naturally they would want to save their own skins.

Then Natty went on. "With powder, I'd stay and fight. But there is only one way to save you. I must reach your father's fort and return with soldiers."

"Of course," Cora said. "I am sure

we can hide here safely until then. Duncan, perhaps you should go too."

"Never," Heyward said firmly.

"I knew you wouldn't," Alice said, touching his arm.

"You would only slow us down anyway," Natty said bluntly. "But enough talking. Time is short."

Natty and Chingachgook began to move out of the cave. But Uncas stayed where he was. He looked at Cora. Cora met his intent gaze.

"I will stay here," Uncas declared. He was speaking directly to Cora.

Cora answered him just as directly. "Please go. *Please.* I will not have you risk your life for nothing."

"She is right," Chingachgook told his son. "You cannot save her by staying here. We must bring back English soldiers. And three of us have a

better chance to do that than two."

Natty laid his hand on Uncas's shoulder. "Your father is right."

"Listen to him," Cora pleaded.

Finally Uncas said, "I will go then. But I will return, I promise you."

"I know you will," Cora said, still looking into his eyes.

Uncas broke off his gaze. He followed the others out of the cave.

Heyward and the women were left there alone. Terribly, fearfully alone.

Chapter 6

Heyward went to the entrance. He looked out. The sky was blue. The July day was bright and hot. Natty and the Mohicans were already out of sight.

Heyward returned to Cora and Alice.

"We can only wait," he said.

"And trust," said Cora.

"And pray," said Alice.

Suddenly they stiffened.

From outside came voices. Indian voices. But Heyward heard a few French words. Words that the French had taught the Indians. *La Longue Carabine. Le Gros Serpent. Le Cerf Agile.*

Heyward knew French well. He understood the words. *The Long Rifle. The Great Serpent. The Swift Deer.*

The Hurons knew whom they were after. They sounded eager for the kill.

"Quick! We must hide fast," Heyward whispered to Cora and Alice.

He led them behind the brushwood that divided the cave. He left only a small gap as a spy hole.

A Huron entered the cave cautiously. He saw no danger. He gave a birdlike whistle. Hurons poured into the cave.

Some were nearly naked. Others wore ragged French uniforms. Some carried rifles. Others carried bows and arrows. All had knives and tomahawks in their belts. All had war paint on their faces.

One came close to the spy hole. Heyward held his breath. He let it out slowly as the Huron turned away. The other Indians were leaving. They had found nothing.

Heyward remembered the second way out of the cave. It was an open hole in the rear. He should stuff it up. No Huron would spot it then.

Heyward signaled to Cora and Alice. They must stay still. He picked up brushwood. He headed for the hole. Bright sunlight shone through it.

Suddenly that light was blotted out. A face appeared. A face lit by fiendish joy. *Magua's face!*

The traitor's face sparked Heyward's rage. He acted without thinking. He dropped the brushwood and whipped out his pistol. He fired—*too late.*

Magua ducked to safety. Even worse, the shot brought the other Hurons running back. This time the brushwood did not fool them.

Heyward's hand tightened on his pistol. Then he stopped himself. He might drop a Huron or two. But others would take revenge on Cora and Alice.

He dropped his weapon and raised his hands. He was herded out of the cave with the women. With them he waited to learn their fate.

A moment later Magua arrived. He walked with a swagger. It was clear he was the Hurons' leader.

He barked a command. The Hurons took Heyward and the women over the rocks into the forest. They moved through the tall pines to a clearing. There Magua halted them. He gave orders. The Hurons gathered vines. They tied Cora, Alice, and Heyward to trees, side by side.

Meanwhile, Heyward had been thinking. There was still hope. They had not been killed on the spot. Maybe Magua was not looking for scalps. Maybe he was looking for ransom.

"You have been most brave, Magua," Heyward began.

"You can call me by my French name," said Magua. *"Le Renard Subtil.* The Cunning Fox."

Heyward kept up his flattery. "You are brave and clever. You kept the Hurons from killing us. Take us now to the fort. Colonel Munro will give you gold for saving his daughters."

Magua smiled like a wolf. "You

think I want gold? That is for white men. They think all things can be bought and sold."

"Medals, too," Heyward promised. "And guns. Powder. Bullets."

"The French give me all I want," said Magua.

Heyward made a last try. Perhaps Magua had a thirst for whiskey. Some Indians had that weakness.

"The colonel will give you what the French will not," Heyward said. "Firewater. As much as you and your men want."

Magua laughed. A chilling laugh.

"Long ago white men gave me firewater," Magua said. "I was a young warrior. Firewater turned me into a baby. My tribe made me leave. It was then that I came to the Mohawks. But I had not escaped the white man's curse. Again I drank. Again I was punished. But not by Indians. This time by an English officer. He did not want Indians to drink. He made an example of me."

Suddenly Magua turned to Cora. "You know the officer. You know what he did to me. You were there. You saw it. I remember it. *Do you?*"

Cora turned pale. "I . . . I think so."

"I *know* so," said Magua fiercely. "You were Colonel Munro's little girl. You saw his men whip me like a dog."

Magua turned to Heyward. "Long have I dreamed of revenge. Now I will have it."

"You cannot kill her for something that happened so long ago," Heyward pleaded.

"Kill her?" said Magua. His chuckle was hideous. "That is not what I

want. The colonel would grieve—
and slowly forget. No. I will have his
daughter as my wife. My willing wife.
So her father can feel the pain his
whole life long."

"I would rather die," said Cora.
Her eyes blazed with defiance.

"And have your sister die?" Magua
asked. "And your major? If you wed
me, I will spare them."

Cora wilted. She bowed her head.

Alice spoke out. Her voice quavered. "Cora, don't do it. I would
rather die than owe my life to *that*."

"Alice speaks for me as well," Heyward said.

"You have your answer," Cora declared.

"Then see your sister die!" Magua
screamed, and flung his tomahawk at
Alice.

It struck the tree above her head

and sliced strands of her golden hair. A huge Huron stepped forward with a knife. He raised it to Alice's throat.

Rage filled Heyward. He snapped the vines that bound him. He charged.

The Huron met Heyward's charge. He wrestled Heyward to the ground. His knees were on Heyward's chest. He raised his knife to plunge it down. Heyward looked up at death.

Chapter 7

Heyward struggled to escape. It was no use. The Huron was too big, too strong. The Huron smiled. His knife flashed.

There was a shot. Then a whizzing sound. The Huron's mouth fell open. Blood spread across his chest. He dropped his knife. He collapsed.

Heyward squirmed out from under him. He saw Natty racing into the clearing. With him were the Mohicans.

"La Longue Carabine!" a Huron screamed.

"Le Gros Serpent! Le Cerf Agile!" shouted others.

"Kill them!" Magua roared.

There was no time to pick up rifles. No time to load and prime them. It was a battle of knives, tomahawks, and bare hands.

Heyward grabbed the tomahawk in the tree above Alice's head and joined in.

Uncas had already killed one Huron with his tomahawk. That evened the odds. Four against four.

Heyward threw his tomahawk at a charging Huron. It glanced off his head. He kept coming. He wrapped giant arms around Heyward in a death hug.

Natty slammed his long rifle against the Huron's head. The Huron went limp.

Meanwhile, Cora had broken

loose. She was trying to free Alice when a Huron seized her. The Huron held Cora's hair in one hand. He bent her neck back. His knife was at her throat.

The sight made Uncas leap like lightning. He slammed into the Huron. They rolled in the dirt. Uncas stood up alone. His knife was in the Huron's heart.

That left only two men fighting—
Chingachgook and Magua.

They wrestled amid the dirt and
fallen leaves. They twisted and
turned. They used all their great
strength. They used all their vast
skill. Neither of them could get the
upper hand.

Then suddenly Chingachgook had
his knife free. He slashed Magua
with it. Magua fell back. He lay like a
corpse.

Chingachgook looked grimly
down at him.

"Finish him," Natty urged.

"But—" Heyward started to pro-
test. This went against his idea of fair
play.

"Here you must kill your enemy,"
Natty said. "Or he will live to kill
you."

Chingachgook raised his knife.

But in a flash Magua was on his feet. He raced into the forest.

"Playing possum." Natty grimaced. "He's a cunning fox indeed."

Chingachgook shrugged. "He's not worth chasing. He has no weapon. He has no help nearby. He cannot hurt us." Chingachgook smiled. "I will have my chance to finish him another time. I can be sure of that."

"Why does he want to kill you so much?" wondered Heyward. "And your son. And Natty, too. He was furious not to catch you in the cave."

Chingachgook merely sneered. It was Natty who explained.

"Long ago, the Mohicans defeated the Hurons in war," Natty said. "They won the Hurons' land. Hurons do not forget or forgive. Magua wants the scalps of the last Mohicans. The scalps would make him a Huron hero. They would wipe away the stain of drink on his name. His dream could come true. He could become chief of the Hurons."

"And what does he want with you?" Heyward asked.

Uncas answered for Natty. "Hawk-eye's scalp alone would make Magua a hero. Hurons speak of the Long Rifle in whispers."

"I can see why," Heyward said. "Your shot saved my life."

"Lucky I still had just enough pow-der for the shot," Natty said. "And lucky we spied the Hurons coming after you. But enough talk. Fort William Henry is a long journey. And who knows what we will find there."

Chapter 8

What they found was trouble.

The first thing Colonel Munro told his daughters was, "Thank the Lord you've reached here alive."

Then he said, "I wish to heaven you had not come.

"We are trapped here," the colonel went on to explain. "The French and their Indians surround us on three sides. The other side is the lake. It is a miracle you managed to get here."

"It was no miracle," said Cora. "It was Mr. Bumppo and his Indian friends. They know every secret trail in the forest."

"And Duncan used his perfect French to trick French soldiers," Alice added.

"If only you could get out of here that easily," Munro said. "Our time is running out."

"We can hold off the French," Heyward declared. "This fort is strong. Our soldiers are brave."

Munro shook his head. "The French have cannons. They are smashing down our walls. Meanwhile they are digging trenches. Every day those trenches come closer. Soon they will be able to attack from them. They have many more men than we. Too many to resist."

"General Webb has fresh troops from England," said Heyward. "And he's an easy march from here."

"He doesn't know we need them," Munro said. "I've sent messengers. None made it through French lines."

Natty stepped forward. "You did not send the right messengers. Give me your message. Webb will get it."

"You saved my daughters," Munro said. "I can't send you back into danger."

"It's no more danger than I'm used to," Natty said.

"I've seen this man in action," Heyward said. "If anyone can get through, Natty can."

"Write your message—and I'll be on my way," Natty said.

Colonel Munro was used to judging men. He looked Natty up and down. Then he wrote his message. He handed it to Natty.

Silently Chingachgook and Uncas moved to Natty's side. Natty shook his head. He spoke to them in Mohican. Uncas started to argue. But he stopped when his father nodded.

"My Indian friends want to go with me," Natty explained. "But a lone man has a better chance of sneaking through. They'll wait here for me."

"We'll be delighted to house them," the colonel said.

"It's the least we can do," said Heyward. "I owe Uncas my life."

"I owe him mine as well," Cora said.

"You must be proud of your son," Munro said to Chingachgook.

"He is young—and sometimes foolish," said Chingachgook. He spoke gruffly, but he could not hide his pride.

Meanwhile, Uncas was looking at Cora. Cora was looking back. Uncas was Indian. Cora was English. The gap between them was big. But something bigger was drawing them together.

Colonel Munro looked at them. He coughed. They broke off their gazes.

"Time for me to go," said Natty.

"I'll have my soldiers start firing," said Munro, getting back to business. "That should distract the French."

Natty went with Munro and Heyward to the walls of the fort. Munro gave orders. Rifles and cannons started to fire. Natty slipped out the gate.

The two officers watched him go. Then Heyward turned to Munro.

"Sir, I want to ask you something," he said. "Before we rejoin the ladies."

Munro smiled. "Could it be about my daughter?"

"Yes, sir," said Heyward.

"I think you will be a fine husband for Cora," Munro said.

Heyward turned slightly red. "Sir, it is Alice I wish to wed."

Munro raised an eyebrow. "I always thought it was Cora you—"

"These last days have shown me how much I love Alice," Heyward said. "She is so gentle, so sweet. She needs someone strong to protect her. Cora does not have that need. She needs a different kind of man."

Munro nodded. "Perhaps you are right. And I'm sure you would make Alice happy. If she says yes, so do I."

"Thank you, sir," Heyward said. "Now I have more reason than ever to hope Natty gets through."

Colonel Munro's face was grim. "God help us all if he doesn't."

Chapter 9

Two days later they saw Natty again. But not the way they hoped.

Natty's face was angry. His arms were tied behind him. His long rifle was gone. And a French officer was at his side.

The Frenchman carried a white flag. It signaled that he had come in peace. He left Natty at the fort gate.

"Open the gate," Colonel Munro commanded. "Let him in."

Once inside, Natty told his story to Munro and Heyward.

"I reached General Webb," said

Natty. "I gave him your message. He wrote one to you. But coming back I was caught." Natty grimaced. "I should have watched my step. The French and Indians are as thick as flies."

"And the message?" asked Munro.

"The French general Montcalm has it," said Natty.

"Do you know what it said?" Heyward asked.

"I didn't read it," said Natty. "But I saw Webb's look when he got your request. Webb looked as if he were taking castor oil. I saw Montcalm's look when he read Webb's answer to you. Montcalm looked pleased as punch. Those looks were clear as deer tracks. They led me to one notion. Webb has told you to swim alone—or sink."

"Impossible!" said Heyward. "No British general would do such a thing."

"That's what you say," Natty said. "But I say that's why Montcalm set me free. He wants you to hear my story. He wants to let you know that

Webb's message is no fake. Because Montcalm is going to slap that message in your face."

Natty was right. Within the hour another Frenchman came under a white flag. General Montcalm wanted to talk with Colonel Munro. The colonel went under the white flag to the French camp. Heyward went along. He could translate what the French commander said.

Montcalm had to say very little to make his point. He merely handed over General Webb's note.

Munro's face darkened when he read it. Webb had written that one English soldier was worth ten French and Indians. He said that Munro needed no more men. So Webb would send no troops. He would not weaken his own defenses.

"Cowardly fool," muttered Munro.

"You have no hope," Montcalm said.

Munro drew himself erect. "No hope, perhaps. But we still have honor. We will not become French prisoners."

Montcalm made a soothing gesture. "You don't have to be. I do not want prisoners. I merely want to destroy your fort. It is on land that we claim. I will let you and all your men march away."

"With our guns? Our uniforms? Our flags?" said Munro.

"With everything—including honor," said Montcalm, smiling.

Munro thought of his men. He thought of his daughters. He looked at Heyward. He flashed a silent question with his eyes. Heyward nodded in reply.

Munro turned to Montcalm. He

gave the only answer he could. "I agree."

Munro and Montcalm shook hands. They saluted. Both were in their dress uniforms. They were perfect pictures of officers and gentlemen.

There was one blot on the picture, though. Near Montcalm stood his Indian allies. Heyward recognized one of them. Magua's eyes met his. Magua smiled. Heyward's blood ran cold.

When Natty heard the news, his face was a picture of disgust. "You think Montcalm will keep his word?" he demanded of Munro.

"Montcalm gave his word of honor," Munro said. "It is something you may not understand."

"I don't know how you fight in Europe," said Natty. "But I know how we fight here. Montcalm's Indians will want scalps. Especially with that devil Magua stirring them up. Montcalm may be a gentleman. But he is still a soldier. He needs those Indians to win this war. And the Indians know it."

Munro shook his head. "The Indians would not dare disobey a general of France." He turned to Heyward. "Do you agree, Major?"

Munro was Heyward's superior. He was Alice's father as well. Heyward tried to forget Magua's smile. "Yes, sir."

Heyward turned to Natty. "You should trust Montcalm, too. He returned your long rifle, didn't he?"

Natty patted his awesome weapon. "It'll be loaded and primed tomorrow," he promised.

Chapter 10

The British troops left the fort with fifes and drums playing. Montcalm had told them they must go back to England. But they could go with honor.

With the British marched local soldiers. By law they were Englishmen, though the English called them colonials. They called themselves Americans.

They marched glumly. They were under English orders. They had to carry unloaded rifles. They did not trust the French. They trusted the Indians still less.

Women and children went, too. They had come to the fort for safety. Now that safety was gone. Cora and Alice rode on horseback among them, soothing fears. They said that Montcalm had given his word. No harm would come.

Three men were not in the march. Natty, Chingachgook, and Uncas. An open road was not for them. They kept to the cover of the trees. But they stayed within earshot of the marching music. They kept their ears open for the first sound of trouble.

It was not long in coming.

The first sound was the whoosh of arrows from the forest on both sides of the road. Then rifle shots. The fifes and drums fell silent. There were screams and groans and desperate commands. Then came the cry of charging Indians.

Confusion swept over the column. Hurons were everywhere. Heyward fought for his life. His sword rose and fell. It parried and thrust. He did not know how long he fought. He lost count of the Indians he downed. Sweat blinded his eyes. His arm felt ready to fall off. Then all was silence. The silence of the grave.

Heyward looked around him. A handful of soldiers stood as dazed as he. The rest lay dead.

Heyward looked at the nearest corpses. He quickly looked away. They were missing their scalps.

Then Heyward saw a horseman approaching. It was Colonel Munro.

The colonel seemed twenty years older and his voice quavered with shock.

"I rode to Montcalm," he said. "I told him to stop it. He said, *'C'est la guerre.'*"

"'It's war,'" Heyward translated automatically. "Natty was right."

"And I was wrong," said Munro. "My God. All these dead. And Cora and Alice missing. We must look for them."

But someone already was. Heyward saw an Indian going through the corpses. His hand tightened on his sword hilt.

Then he saw who it was. "Uncas," he said.

Natty and Chingachgook came out of the forest. They joined the two officers.

"We came as fast as we could," Natty said. "But there was not much we could do. My deerslayer bagged a few, though. And Uncas jumped right into the fight."

Chingachgook shook his head. "He wanted to save your women. One especially. The dark-haired one. His blood runs hot with youth."

Uncas returned from his search. "Cora and Alice are not here," he said. "But I found their trail."

The others followed him. He showed where a glove of Cora's lay. He followed the footprints of two pairs of small feet.

"Women's feet," Uncas said. "See how lightly they tread? And look at these."

He pointed to other footprints. Larger and deeper.

"An Indian," remarked Natty.

"Magua," said Uncas.

"Surely you can't tell that from a footprint," Heyward said.

"Each man walks his own way," Uncas said. "I followed his trail that time he captured you. I do not forget tracks."

Natty patted his shoulder. "Soon you'll be a better woodsman than I am."

"We must catch up with them," said Munro. "Free them from that devil."

Natty shook his head. "The sun is setting. It will be too dark to follow the trail. We must wait until morning."

"By that time they'll have gone too far," Munro protested.

"Maybe so," Natty said. "But there is no help for it. There's no stopping the sunset. There's no hurrying the sunrise. And we'll still have a chance to catch them. If you're willing to take a gamble. And do what I say."

"What choice do we have?" asked Heyward.

The colonel nodded. "You're in command, Mr. Bumppo. Or should I call you by your other name? The name that fits you better. Hawkeye."

Chapter 11

They slept in the ruins of the fort.
The French had burned it to the
ground.

Natty shook Heyward and Munro
awake. The stars were still out. But
the east was pale with dawn.

"A whole night lost," groaned
Munro. "How can we make up that
time?"

"We'll do more than read Magua's
trail," said Natty. "We'll read his
mind.

"Magua will go north—to the
Hurons," Natty continued. "He wants

to show his people English scalps. And Englishwomen. He wants to be a hero. Even more, he wants to be a chief."

"So we know he's going north," said Heyward. "What good does that do us? He is still far ahead of us."

"His way north runs along Lake George," said Natty. "We can canoe it. We'll make much better time than Magua. He's on foot. The women will slow him down still more. The trail we found yesterday told us that."

Natty led the Englishmen to the lake. Chingachgook and Uncas were waiting there. The Mohicans had bargained with local Indians. They had a long canoe.

They got into the canoe. Natty, the Mohicans, and Heyward took paddles. Colonel Munro sat in the center. He looked old and frail. The deaths of his men wounded him. The loss of his daughters ate at his heart.

They pushed off. The canoe cut through the water as the rising sun lit the lake. The water sparkled like a million jewels. Heyward was dazzled. This was one of the most beautiful spots on earth.

Suddenly he stiffened. The beauty vanished. A war canoe was coming from the shore. It was filled with Indians.

"Hurons," said Natty. "Paddle faster."

But the Hurons kept gaining.

Natty thrust his paddle into Munro's hands. "Can you help?"

Strength flooded back into the colonel. "Of course," he said. He dug his paddle hard into the water.

Natty picked up his long rifle. "They think they're safe at this distance. They don't know my deer-slayer."

He raised his rifle. He barely seemed to aim it. He squeezed the trigger. In the far-off canoe a Huron clutched his chest. He fell into the water.

Heyward smiled. The Hurons had a new tale to tell about *la Longue Carabine.*

Natty reloaded. He raised his rifle again. Another shot. Another Huron toppled over.

Natty put down his rifle. "That's enough. No sense wasting powder."

He was right. The race was over. They left the Hurons out of sight.

It was afternoon when they reached the end of the lake. Their muscles ached. Sweat soaked their clothes. But Uncas bounded out of the canoe.

He was the first into the forest. He was leading the search for Magua's trail. His shout brought the others running.

With a fallen log he had changed the course of a shallow stream. He wanted to see its bottom. In the streambed were footprints. Two pairs were small.

"Hats off to you, youngster," said Natty. "You make me feel as if my eyes were getting old."

Even Chingachgook could not keep back a smile. "You show promise, my son," he said.

Uncas was already moving ahead. The hard part had been picking up the trail. The rest would be easy.

It was. They swiftly followed the trail the rest of the day. They slept in the forest that night. At dawn they started again. It was late afternoon when an Indian village came into sight. The village was large. Its huts were made of earth, with rounded roofs.

"We have to watch our step," Natty said. "We don't know what tribe this is."

Uncas was already crawling toward the village. Soon he returned.

"It is a tribe of the Delaware," he reported. "On a blanket I saw the tribe totem. The tortoise."

Heyward smiled. "Then we can get help. You told me the Mohicans once ruled the Delaware."

Chingachgook's face was grim. "That was long ago. Men forget fast. And the tribes of the Delaware are like fallen leaves. They are scattered wide. Many fight for the French.

They are on the side of their old foes. The Hurons."

"Magua may even have stopped here," Natty said. "He may still be here."

"I will find out," Uncas said. Before anyone could stop him, he was gone.

"Too hotheaded," said his father, shaking his head.

"And too warm-hearted, I think," said Natty. "When he thinks of Cora." Natty shrugged. "We can only wait. And hope he returns."

Chapter 12

Darkness fell. Owls hooted. A sliver of a moon moved through the stars. But Uncas did not return.

No one slept that night. At sunrise Natty said, "We must go into the village after him."

He turned to Heyward. "Change out of your uniform. I have spare clothes. You can be a French trapper. You speak the language."

Then he said to Chingachgook, "Stay here. Protect the colonel. Don't worry. I'll get Uncas out."

Chingachgook nodded. "I trust you, Hawkeye."

Natty handed the Mohican his long rifle. "I trust you, too, old friend. Keep my deerslayer safe. I can't take it with me. Indians know it too well."

Natty carried Chingachgook's rifle into the village. Heyward carried a rifle, too. But they were met by a dozen Delaware rifles and more.

Heyward raised his hand in peace. "I come from your French father in Quebec," he said in French.

"Welcome," an Indian answered in French. From his manner, he was a chief. "You are our guests."

Heyward took out trinkets. Colored glass beads, buttons, and sewing needles. He held them out to the chief. But then he almost dropped them.

He saw Cora.

She was standing between two Indian women. Heyward blessed her quick wits. She gave no sign of knowing him.

He handed the trinkets to the chief. "I see you have another guest," he said.

The chief grunted. "No guest. A prisoner. An enemy. English."

"Let me question her," Heyward said. "She may know something useful."

The chief frowned. "No use. I have tried. She speaks no French."

"I speak English," Heyward said.

"Good luck then," the chief said.

Heyward and Natty went to Cora. There was no time to waste words.

"Tell me what happened," Heyward said.

"Magua left me here," Cora said. "These Indians are his allies. Magua was worried about Mr. Bumppo and his friends. They might chase and catch him. Then he could use me as a hostage. He could make them let him go. Or else he would have me killed."

"A cunning fox, indeed," Heyward said. He swallowed hard. "What has he done with Alice?"

"He took her with him," Cora said. "That way he kept power over me. I would not try to escape."

"Where did he go?" asked Natty.

"To a Huron village," said Cora. "It is nearby. He wanted to get warriors to protect him and his prizes. Then he would return for me."

"We have to get you out of here fast," said Heyward.

"Not only me," said Cora. "Uncas."

"You know what happened to him then?" Natty asked eagerly.

"They caught him sneaking into

the village last night," Cora said. "They called him a spy. They tortured him. But he would not say a word. They have him in a hut under guard."

"Brave lad," said Natty. "We must get him out, too."

"But how?" Cora asked.

"I'll think of some—" Natty began.

That was as far as he got.

A whoop of triumph split the air.

Magua stood pointing at his enemies.

Behind him stood twenty Hurons. All had rifles primed. Behind him, too, stood Alice. She was pale and trembling.

Heyward did not know the Huron language. But he knew what Magua had screamed out:

"Kill them!"

Chapter 13

"Stop!" the Delaware chief ordered Magua. He spoke in French. The Hurons did not know the Delaware tongue. "These are our guests. They are safe from harm in our village."

Magua looked around him. The Delaware men had raised their rifles.

"These are foes of the French father," Magua said. "An English major. And the famous Yankee hunter. *La Longue Carabine*. His scalp is worth much."

A murmur went up. Delawares

crowded around Natty to look at him.

"Still they are guests," said the chief.

"If you spare them, the French father will be angry," said Magua. "He will make war on you. And the Hurons will help him destroy you."

The Delaware chief was torn. Was honor worth the risk? "Tamenund must decide," he announced.

Another murmur went up. Heyward turned to Natty. "Who is Tamenund?"

"The oldest of the old. The wisest of the wise," Natty said. "No one knows how old. But everyone knows how wise."

Tamenund was very old. He needed two sticks to walk from his hut. He was shrunken in his rich robes.

His face was all wrinkles. But his eyes were clear.

"Let both sides speak," he said. His voice cracked with age. "In the tongue they choose. I have learned many tongues. The harsh tongues of tribes that once were enemies. The forked tongues of whites who called themselves friends."

Magua stepped boldly forward. "Give me these two lives," he said in Huron. "The French will give many guns in return. And I will give you a promise. The one that I gave my people. I will take many more English scalps. I will sweep the English away. Make me chief, as the Hurons have, and you will have your own land again."

Tamenund nodded. "And now the other side," he said.

Natty stepped forward. "White

men's tongues are clumsy," he said in English. "They cloud the truth. Listen to one of your own people. One who speaks with the voice of truth itself."

"Where is he?" Tamenund asked.

"You hold him captive," Natty said.

Tamenund looked at the Delaware chief.

"We caught a spy last night," the chief explained. "He would not say a word to us—despite all we could do."

"Bring him here," Tamenund said. "Perhaps he will speak now."

Uncas was brought to them. His clothes were torn. His face was bruised. But he walked tall and proud.

"What is your tongue?" Tamenund asked.

"The same as yours," Uncas replied. "The tongue of my fathers.

And their fathers—back to the beginning of time."

Tamenund's bent body seemed to straighten. His voice quivered with excitement. "Your voice is like music. What is your name?"

"Uncas," the young man answered.

"Your father?" asked Tamenund.

"Chingachgook," Uncas said.

"Your tribe?" asked Tamenund.

"The Mohican," Uncas said.

"Your proof?" Tamenund demanded.

Silently Uncas ripped open his shirt. A tattoo gleamed on his bare chest.

Beside Natty, Cora said, "What is it?"

"The sacred tortoise," Natty said. "The ruling totem of the Delaware."

Tamenund laid his withered hand on Uncas's broad shoulder. "I thank

the Great Spirit that I live to see this day. I have seen our people lose their greatness. But now I see hope return. I see the noble son of the noblest tribe. A tribe I feared had vanished from the earth. Only a Mohican chief can bring our scattered people together."

Magua could not hold himself back. "Old fool!" he shouted. He turned to the Delawares. "Listen to me. I will bring you guns, gold, glory!"

The Delaware chief leveled his rifle. "Silence, Huron dog. You are a guest. Otherwise you would die."

Magua looked around him. He and his men were outnumbered. "I will leave you fools then," he snarled. "Give me the woman I left with you."

"Never!" Uncas spat out.

Magua turned to Tamenund. "I

demand justice from you."

"You came with just one woman to-day," Tamenund said. "You will leave with just one."

Cora stepped forward. "I will be that one," she declared. "Leave Alice here."

"No!" Alice screamed. "I won't let you!"

But Magua had already grabbed Cora's arm. "I knew I would have you in the end. You will be my queen."

Uncas started forward. Tamenund's hand tightened on his shoulder. "You are a great chief. But our law is greater."

Chapter 14

"Dogs, rabbits, thieves—I spit on you!"

Those were Magua's parting words. Then he took Cora and led her and his men out of the village.

Uncas shook free of Tamenund. "Men of the Delaware! Do you take me as your leader?" he demanded.

The Delawares shouted that they did.

"Then pick up your rifles and follow me," Uncas said. "We will show Magua who is the dog, the rabbit, the thief."

"Wait for me, Uncas," said Natty. "I'll get my deerslayer."

"And I my pistol," Heyward said.

They ran to where Chingachgook and Munro waited in the forest. Quickly they explained what happened.

Soon the colonel had joined Alice in the village. Heyward, Chingachgook, and Natty joined Uncas and his warriors.

Chingachgook watched Uncas at their head. He nodded. "My son has become a chief. As he was born to be."

They had to wait until Magua was off Delaware land. Then they were free of the sacred law. They could give chase.

"A child could follow their trail," said Uncas. "They are as clumsy as cattle. And they move like snails."

His look was angry. "Cora slows them down."

"They're heading for the hills," said Natty. "Where there are caves to hide in. And rocks to shield them in a fight."

Natty was right. Soon they saw cliffs through breaks in the trees. Then they saw Magua.

Magua led his band up a hillside trail. He was dragging Cora by the hand.

That was all Uncas had to see. "Wait here," he told the others. "I will deal with Magua myself."

He was off like a flash. He lived up to his name. He ran as swift as a deer.

"He's mad," Heyward muttered.

"No," said Natty. "Just too worried about Cora. He fears for her if we all attack."

"He is a Mohican," Chingachgook said. His eyes were sad. But his voice was proud. "He laughs at danger."

Minutes passed. They seemed to last forever. Then Uncas came into view. He was on a cliff above Magua.

Meanwhile Magua had stopped. He was arguing with Cora. It was clear why. She had to move faster. He seized her hand. But she did not move. He raised his knife. She kept her feet planted.

"He'll kill her," Heyward said. He started to run forward. Natty and the others joined him.

But Magua hesitated. He did not want to kill her—and kill his dream. He still saw her as his queen.

A Huron warrior beside him saw her differently. She meant death to them all. His knife flashed.

Uncas whooped—and leaped. He

was too late. The Huron's knife was buried in Cora. And Magua's knife plunged into the murderer.

Uncas landed on his hands and knees. Magua swiftly turned. His knife rose and plunged again.

Uncas lay beside Cora. They were joined in death.

Racing forward, Chingachgook gave a terrible shriek. Magua heard it. He started running. His men ran for their lives as well.

Suddenly Magua stopped. The trail ended. He faced a deep chasm. On the other side lay safety. He crouched. He leaped the gap.

He almost made it.

His feet fell inches short. But his hands grabbed the top of the ledge. Slowly he started to pull himself up.

A shot rang out.

Magua shuddered. His hands let

go. His body fell to the rocks far below. There it lay lifeless.

Natty stood with his long rifle smoking. But he felt no joy. Around him the battle was over. Many Hurons lay dead. The rest had fled. There was nothing left to do except carry Cora and Uncas back to the village.

That evening Cora and Uncas lay side by side again—in the sacred burying ground of the Delaware.

"It is fitting," Chingachgook said, gazing at their graves. "The woman had the heart of a Mohican. She was worthy of the heart of my son."

"Will you now lead the Delaware?" asked Heyward.

Chingachgook shook his head. "Uncas was like the rising sun. He could have led his people to a new day. But my sun is setting. I will go to the land of the setting sun. Long ago the Mohicans came from there. And there the sun still shines on my race. May it do so until my days are done."

"And I'll go with you," said Natty. "I see too many farms here. Too many fences. Too many roads. Too many towns. My parents came from England. But I am a son of the wilderness. I need freedom as I need air to breathe."

"I only want to go back to England," Alice said. "Cora was made for this new land. But I am not."

"I'll join you there," said Heyward. "After I help your father to win this war. I don't belong here either. England may claim this place. But the people here are not English. I am not sure what they are. Or how long the British flag will fly over them."

Heyward looked at Natty standing

tall. He looked at the long rifle in Natty's hand. "I hope I do not have to fight for that flag again in these colonies," he said.

Then they fell silent. The Delawares around them fell silent, too. Tamenund was saying final words over the graves of Cora and Uncas.

"The palefaces are masters of the earth. The time of the red men has not yet come again. My day has been too long. In the morning I saw the sons of the tortoise happy and strong. Yet before the night has come, I have lived to see the last warrior of the wise race of the Mohicans."

Historical Note

The British finally did defeat the French. At the end of 1759 the British army captured Quebec in Canada. The French general Montcalm died in that battle. With this victory the British won the war. The peace treaty gave them Canada.

In 1775, however, the thirteen colonies below Canada rebelled against British rule. The war that followed, the American Revolution, lasted until 1783. It ended in British defeat—and in the birth of the United States of America.

Les Martin is the author and adapter of many books for children, including *The Time Machine* and *Oliver Twist*, both Step-Up Classics™, and *The Vampire*, a Step-Up Classic Chiller™. An avid tennis player, Les Martin lives in New York City.

Shannon Stirnweis is a painter and illustrator with dozens of books to his credit. He likes to paint wilderness scenes, so he especially enjoyed working on *The Last of the Mohicans*. Born in Oregon, Shannon Stirnweis now lives in Wilton, Connecticut, with his wife and son.